W9-AFP-417

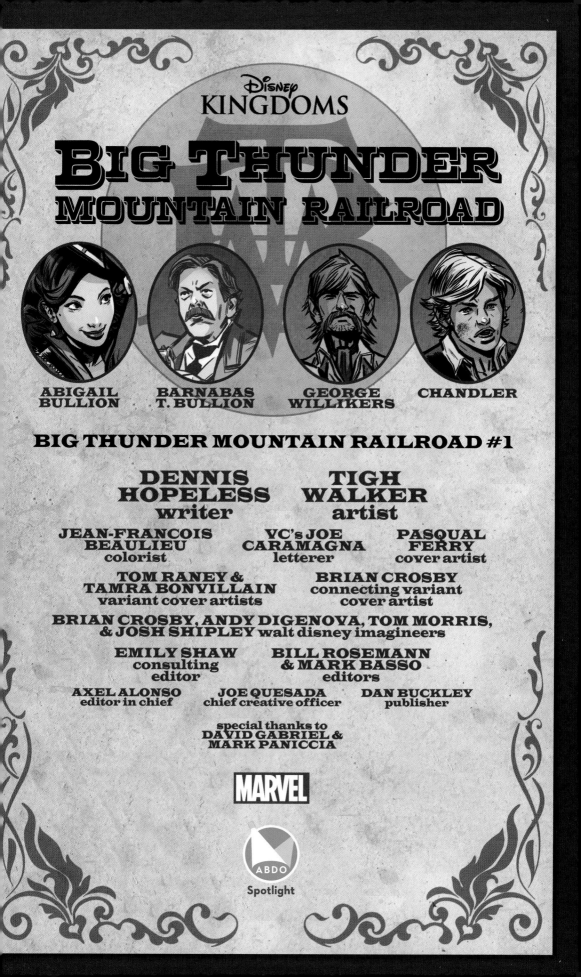

DISNEY KINGDOMS

BIG THUNDER
MOUNTAIN RAILROAD

ABIGAIL BULLION

BARNABAS T. BULLION

GEORGE WILLIKERS

CHANDLER

BIG THUNDER MOUNTAIN RAILROAD #1

DENNIS HOPELESS
writer

TIGH WALKER
artist

JEAN-FRANCOIS BEAULIEU
colorist

VC's JOE CARAMAGNA
letterer

PASQUAL FERRY
cover artist

TOM RANEY & TAMRA BONVILLAIN
variant cover artists

BRIAN CROSBY
connecting variant cover artist

BRIAN CROSBY, ANDY DIGENOVA, TOM MORRIS, & JOSH SHIPLEY walt disney imagineers

EMILY SHAW
consulting editor

BILL ROSEMANN & MARK BASSO
editors

AXEL ALONSO
editor in chief

JOE QUESADA
chief creative officer

DAN BUCKLEY
publisher

special thanks to
DAVID GABRIEL & MARK PANICCIA

MARVEL

ABDO
Spotlight

ABDOPUBLISHING.COM

Reinforced library bound edition published in 2017 by Spotlight,
a division of ABDO, PO Box 398166, Minneapolis, Minnesota 55439.
Spotlight produces high-quality reinforced library bound editions for
schools and libraries. Published by agreement with Marvel Characters, Inc.

Printed in the United States of America, North Mankato, Minnesota.
092016
012017

marvelkids.com

© 2015 MARVEL

**Elements based on Walt Disney's
Big Thunder Mountain Railroad © Disney.**

PUBLISHER'S CATALOGING IN PUBLICATION DATA

Names: Hopeless, Dennis, author. I Walker, Tigh ; Beaulieu, Jean-Francois ; Ruiz, Felix ;
    Mogorron, Guillermo, illustrators.
Title: Big Thunder Mountain Railroad / writer: Dennis Hopeless ; art: Tigh Walker ;
    Jean-Francois Beaulieu ; Felix Ruiz ; Guillermo Mogorron.
Description: Reinforced library bound edition. I Minneapolis, Minnesota : Spotlight, 2017. I
    Series: Disney Kingdoms: Big Thunder Mountain Railroad I Volumes 1, 2 and 4 written by
    Dennis Hopeless ; illustrated by Tigh Walker & Jean-Francois Beaulieu. I Volume 3 written
    by Dennis Hopeless ; illustrated by Felix Ruiz & Jean-Francois Beaulieu. I Volume 5 written
    by Dennis Hopeless ; illustrated by Tigh Walker, Guillermo Mogorron & Jean-Francois
    Beaulieu.
Summary: When Abby traveled west to Rainbow Ridge to live with her father Barnabas T.
    Bullion at the Big Thunder Mountain gold mine, the brave young hero never thought
    she'd join a group of bandits to rob her own father's mine.
Identifiers: LCCN 2016941684 I ISBN 9781614795759 (v.1 ; lib. bdg.) I ISBN 9781614795766
    (v.2 ; lib. bdg.) I ISBN 9781614795773 (v.3 ; lib. bdg.) I ISBN 9781614795780 (v.4 ; lib.
    bdg.) I ISBN 9781614795797 (v.5 ; lib. bdg.)
Subjects: Disney (Fictitious characters)--Juvenile fiction. I Adventures and adventurers--Juvenile
    fiction. I Graphic novels--Juvenile fiction.
Classification: DDC 741.5--dc23
LC record available at https://lccn.loc.gov/2016941684

Spotlight

A Division of ABDO
abdopublishing.com

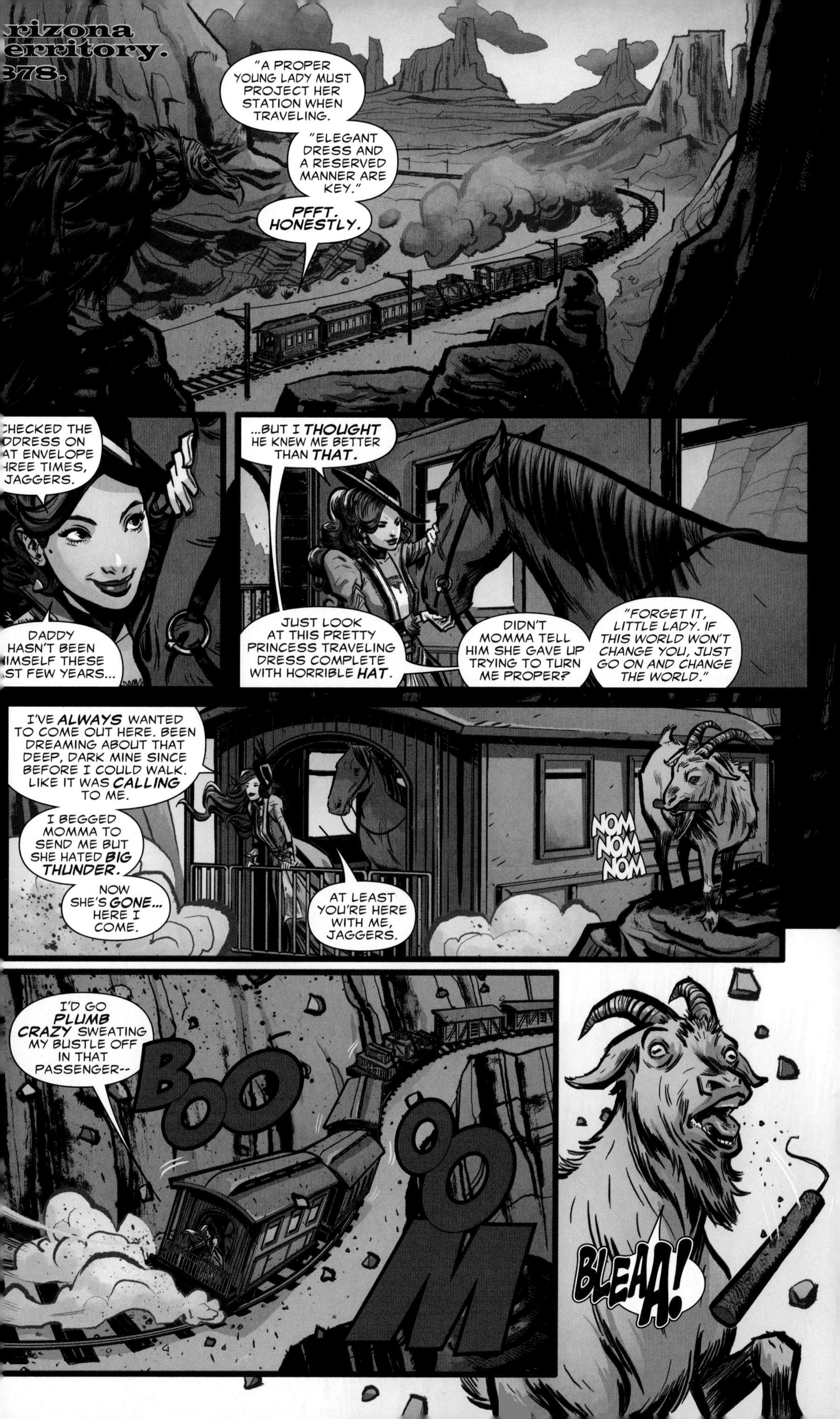
rizona
erritory.
378.
"A PROPER YOUNG LADY MUST PROJECT HER STATION WHEN TRAVELING.
"ELEGANT DRESS AND A RESERVED MANNER ARE KEY."
PFFT. HONESTLY.
HECKED THE DDRESS ON AT ENVELOPE HREE TIMES, JAGGERS.
DADDY HASN'T BEEN IMSELF THESE ST FEW YEARS...
...BUT I THOUGHT HE KNEW ME BETTER THAN THAT.
JUST LOOK AT THIS PRETTY PRINCESS TRAVELING DRESS COMPLETE WITH HORRIBLE HAT.
DIDN'T MOMMA TELL HIM SHE GAVE UP TRYING TO TURN ME PROPER?
"FORGET IT, LITTLE LADY. IF THIS WORLD WON'T CHANGE YOU, JUST GO ON AND CHANGE THE WORLD."
I'VE ALWAYS WANTED TO COME OUT HERE. BEEN DREAMING ABOUT THAT DEEP, DARK MINE SINCE BEFORE I COULD WALK. LIKE IT WAS CALLING TO ME.
I BEGGED MOMMA TO SEND ME BUT SHE HATED BIG THUNDER.
NOW SHE'S GONE... HERE I COME.
AT LEAST YOU'RE HERE WITH ME, JAGGERS.
NOM NOM NOM
I'D GO PLUMB CRAZY SWEATING MY BUSTLE OFF IN THAT PASSENGER--
BOOOOM
BLEAA!

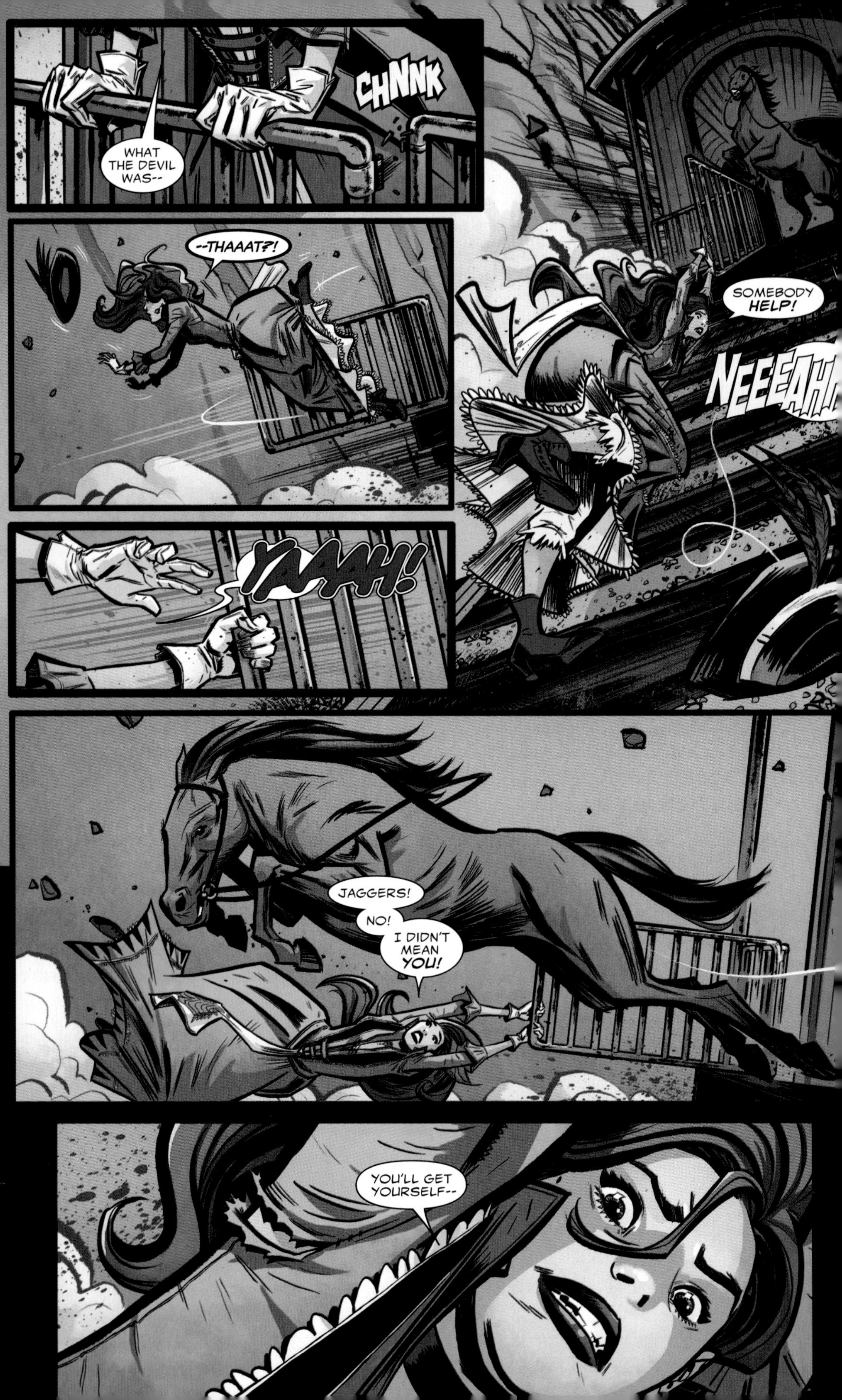

CHNNK
WHAT THE DEVIL WAS--
--THAAAT?!
SOMEBODY HELP!
NEEEAHH
YAAAH!
JAGGERS!
NO!
I DIDN'T MEAN YOU!
YOU'LL GET YOURSELF--

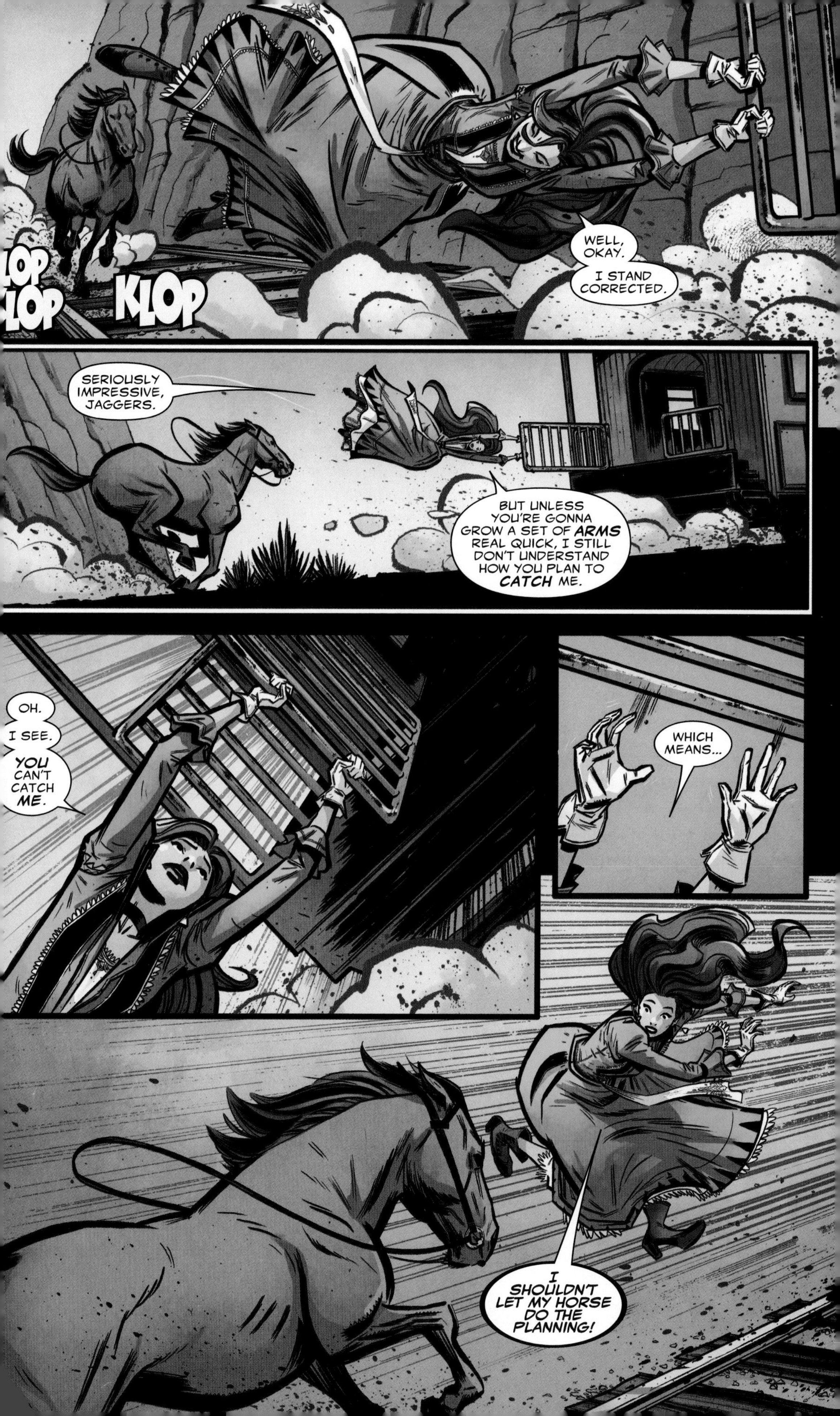
KLOP
KLOP
KLOP
WELL, OKAY.
I STAND CORRECTED.
SERIOUSLY IMPRESSIVE, JAGGERS.
BUT UNLESS YOU'RE GONNA GROW A SET OF ARMS REAL QUICK, I STILL DON'T UNDERSTAND HOW YOU PLAN TO CATCH ME.
OH.
I SEE.
YOU CAN'T CATCH ME.
WHICH MEANS...
I SHOULDN'T LET MY HORSE DO THE PLANNING!

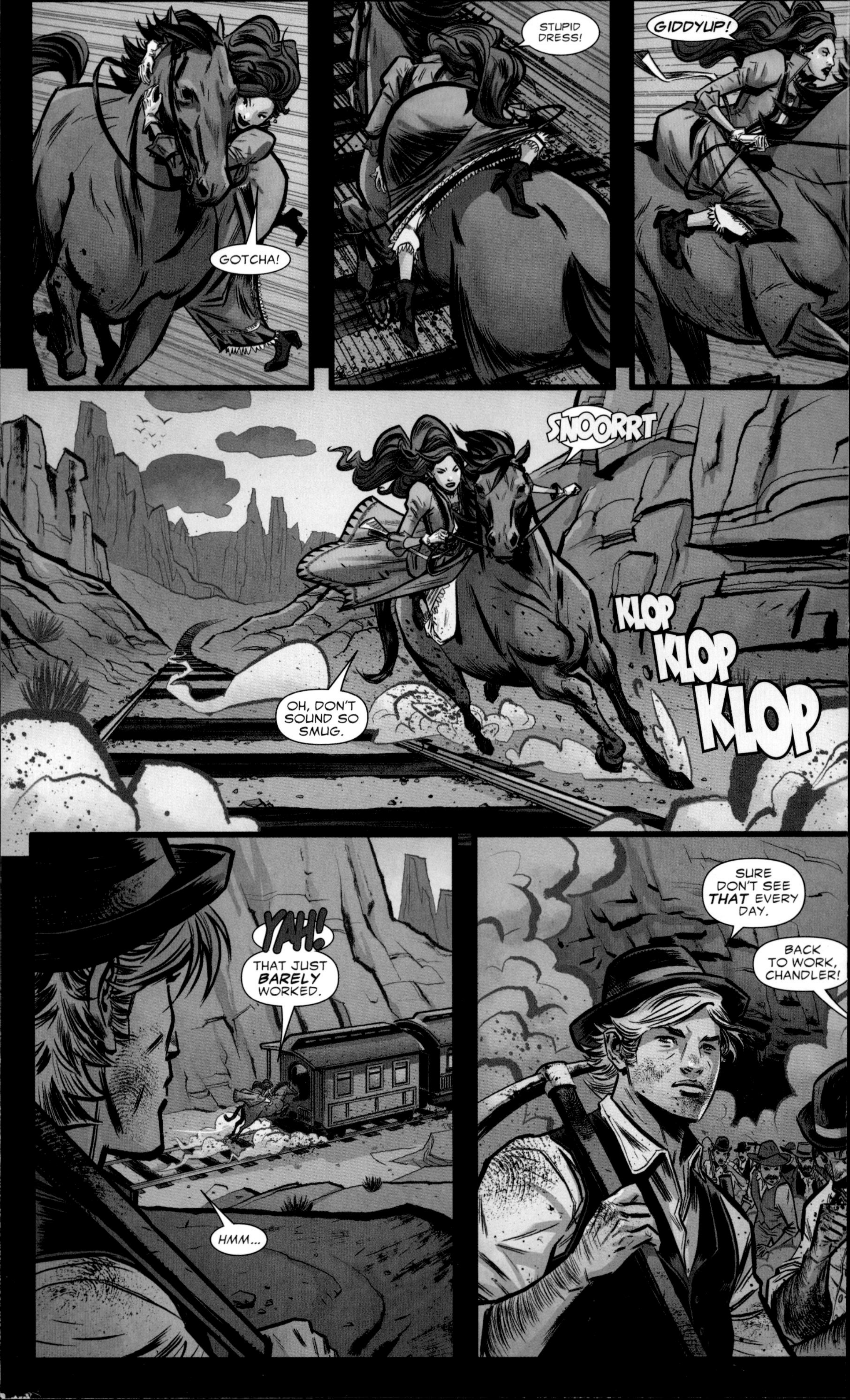
GOTCHA!
STUPID DRESS!
GIDDYUP!
SNOORRT
OH, DON'T SOUND SO SMUG.
KLOP
KLOP
KLOP
YAH!
THAT JUST *BARELY* WORKED.
HMM...
SURE DON'T SEE *THAT* EVERY DAY.
BACK TO WORK, CHANDLER!

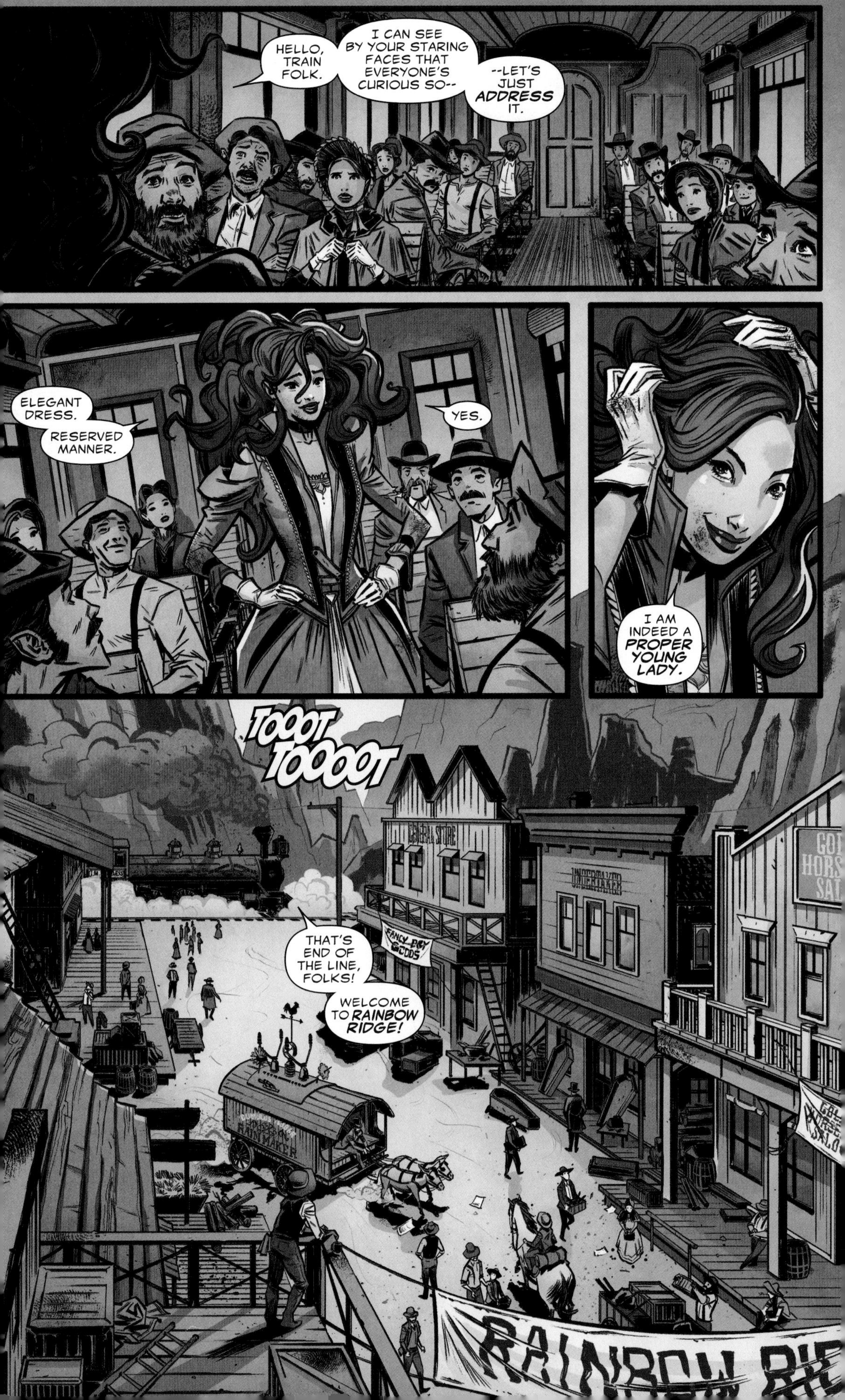
HELLO, TRAIN FOLK.
I CAN SEE BY YOUR STARING FACES THAT EVERYONE'S CURIOUS SO--
--LET'S JUST ADDRESS IT.
ELEGANT DRESS.
RESERVED MANNER.
YES.
I AM INDEED A PROPER YOUNG LADY.
TOOOT TOOOOT
GENERAL STORE
UNDERTAKER
THAT'S END OF THE LINE, FOLKS!
WELCOME TO RAINBOW RIDGE!
RAINMAKER

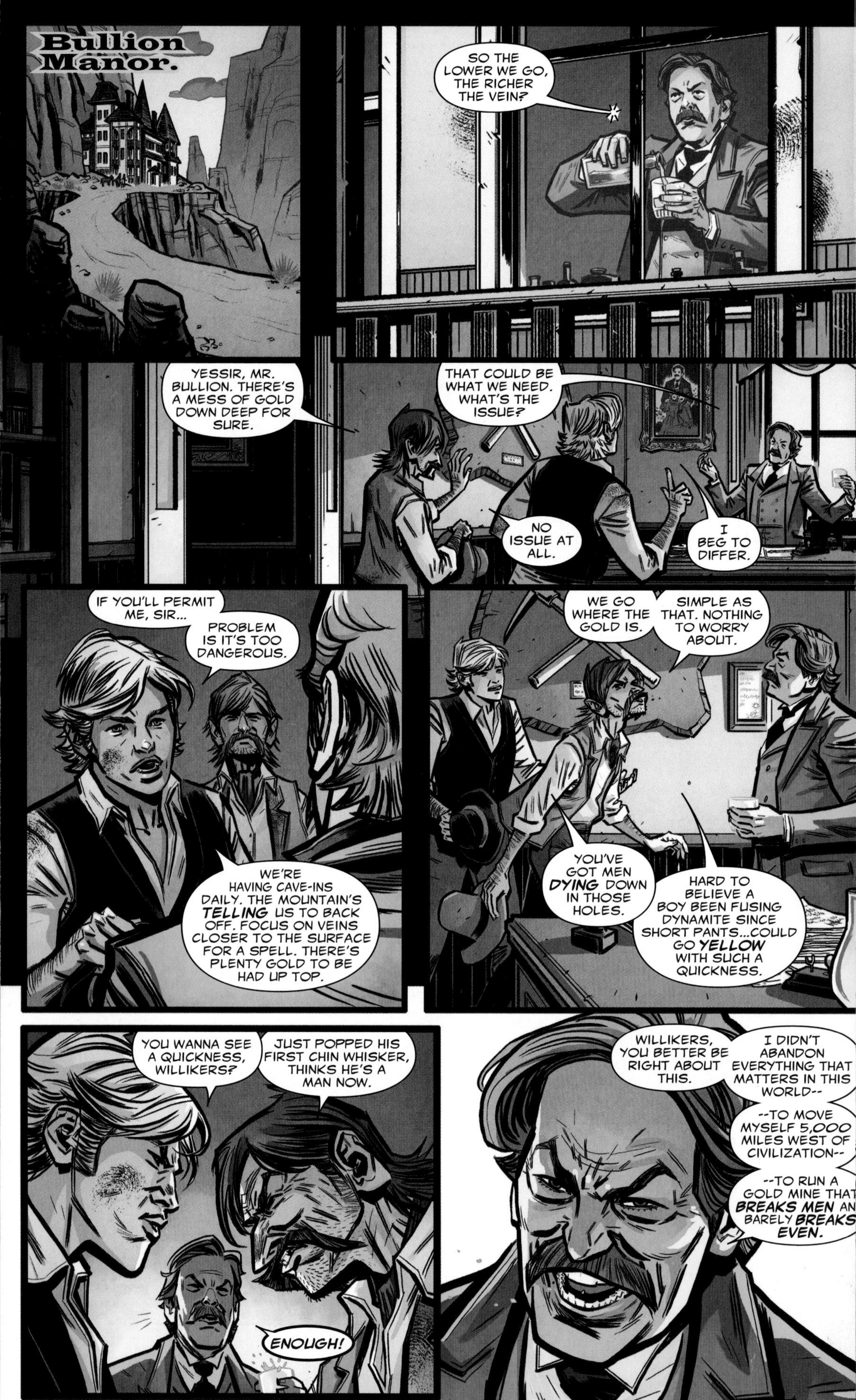
Bullion Manor.
SO THE LOWER WE GO, THE RICHER THE VEIN?
YESSIR, MR. BULLION. THERE'S A MESS OF GOLD DOWN DEEP FOR SURE.
THAT COULD BE WHAT WE NEED. WHAT'S THE ISSUE?
NO ISSUE AT ALL.
I BEG TO DIFFER.
IF YOU'LL PERMIT ME, SIR...
PROBLEM IS IT'S TOO DANGEROUS.
WE'RE HAVING CAVE-INS DAILY. THE MOUNTAIN'S TELLING US TO BACK OFF. FOCUS ON VEINS CLOSER TO THE SURFACE FOR A SPELL. THERE'S PLENTY GOLD TO BE HAD UP TOP.
WE GO WHERE THE GOLD IS.
SIMPLE AS THAT. NOTHING TO WORRY ABOUT.
YOU'VE GOT MEN DYING DOWN IN THOSE HOLES.
HARD TO BELIEVE A BOY BEEN FUSING DYNAMITE SINCE SHORT PANTS...COULD GO YELLOW WITH SUCH A QUICKNESS.
YOU WANNA SEE A QUICKNESS, WILLIKERS?
JUST POPPED HIS FIRST CHIN WHISKER, THINKS HE'S A MAN NOW.
ENOUGH!
WILLIKERS, YOU BETTER BE RIGHT ABOUT THIS.
I DIDN'T ABANDON EVERYTHING THAT MATTERS IN THIS WORLD--
--TO MOVE MYSELF 5,000 MILES WEST OF CIVILIZATION--
--TO RUN A GOLD MINE THAT BREAKS MEN AN BARELY BREAKS EVEN.

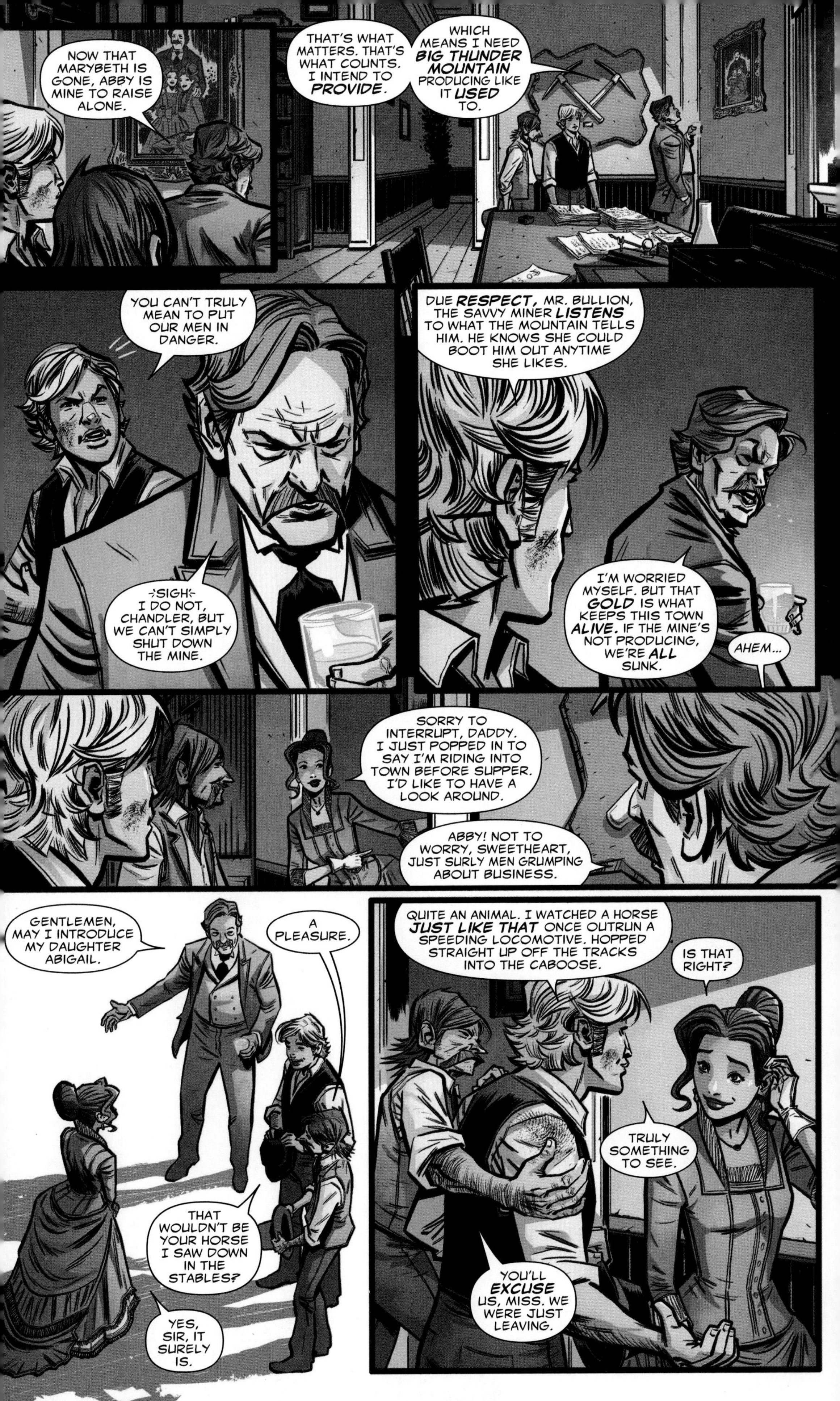
NOW THAT MARYBETH IS GONE, ABBY IS MINE TO RAISE ALONE.
THAT'S WHAT MATTERS. THAT'S WHAT COUNTS. I INTEND TO PROVIDE.
WHICH MEANS I NEED BIG THUNDER MOUNTAIN PRODUCING LIKE IT USED TO.
YOU CAN'T TRULY MEAN TO PUT OUR MEN IN DANGER.
SIGH
I DO NOT, CHANDLER, BUT WE CAN'T SIMPLY SHUT DOWN THE MINE.
DUE RESPECT, MR. BULLION, THE SAVVY MINER LISTENS TO WHAT THE MOUNTAIN TELLS HIM. HE KNOWS SHE COULD BOOT HIM OUT ANYTIME SHE LIKES.
I'M WORRIED MYSELF. BUT THAT GOLD IS WHAT KEEPS THIS TOWN ALIVE. IF THE MINE'S NOT PRODUCING, WE'RE ALL SUNK.
AHEM...
SORRY TO INTERRUPT, DADDY. I JUST POPPED IN TO SAY I'M RIDING INTO TOWN BEFORE SUPPER. I'D LIKE TO HAVE A LOOK AROUND.
ABBY! NOT TO WORRY, SWEETHEART, JUST SURLY MEN GRUMPING ABOUT BUSINESS.
GENTLEMEN, MAY I INTRODUCE MY DAUGHTER ABIGAIL.
A PLEASURE.
THAT WOULDN'T BE YOUR HORSE I SAW DOWN IN THE STABLES?
YES, SIR, IT SURELY IS.
QUITE AN ANIMAL. I WATCHED A HORSE JUST LIKE THAT ONCE OUTRUN A SPEEDING LOCOMOTIVE. HOPPED STRAIGHT UP OFF THE TRACKS INTO THE CABOOSE.
IS THAT RIGHT?
TRULY SOMETHING TO SEE.
YOU'LL EXCUSE US, MISS. WE WERE JUST LEAVING.

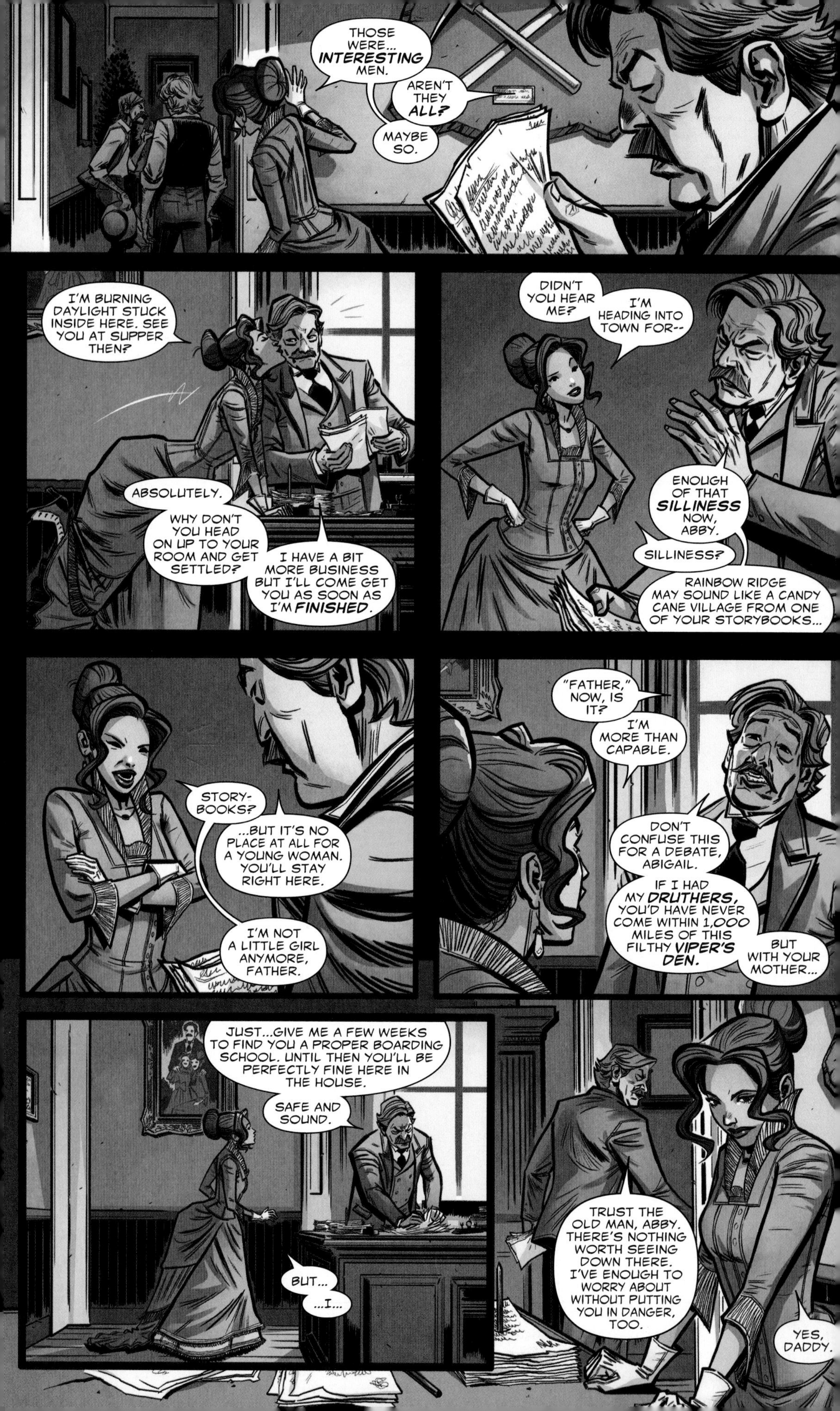

THOSE WERE... INTERESTING MEN.
AREN'T THEY ALL?
MAYBE SO.
I'M BURNING DAYLIGHT STUCK INSIDE HERE. SEE YOU AT SUPPER THEN?
ABSOLUTELY.
WHY DON'T YOU HEAD ON UP TO YOUR ROOM AND GET SETTLED?
I HAVE A BIT MORE BUSINESS BUT I'LL COME GET YOU AS SOON AS I'M FINISHED.
DIDN'T YOU HEAR ME?
I'M HEADING INTO TOWN FOR--
ENOUGH OF THAT SILLINESS NOW, ABBY.
SILLINESS?
RAINBOW RIDGE MAY SOUND LIKE A CANDY CANE VILLAGE FROM ONE OF YOUR STORYBOOKS...
STORY-BOOKS?
...BUT IT'S NO PLACE AT ALL FOR A YOUNG WOMAN. YOU'LL STAY RIGHT HERE.
I'M NOT A LITTLE GIRL ANYMORE, FATHER.
"FATHER," NOW, IS IT?
I'M MORE THAN CAPABLE.
DON'T CONFUSE THIS FOR A DEBATE, ABIGAIL.
IF I HAD MY DRUTHERS, YOU'D HAVE NEVER COME WITHIN 1,000 MILES OF THIS FILTHY VIPER'S DEN.
BUT WITH YOUR MOTHER...
JUST...GIVE ME A FEW WEEKS TO FIND YOU A PROPER BOARDING SCHOOL. UNTIL THEN YOU'LL BE PERFECTLY FINE HERE IN THE HOUSE.
SAFE AND SOUND.
BUT...
...I...
TRUST THE OLD MAN, ABBY. THERE'S NOTHING WORTH SEEING DOWN THERE. I'VE ENOUGH TO WORRY ABOUT WITHOUT PUTTING YOU IN DANGER, TOO.
YES, DADDY.

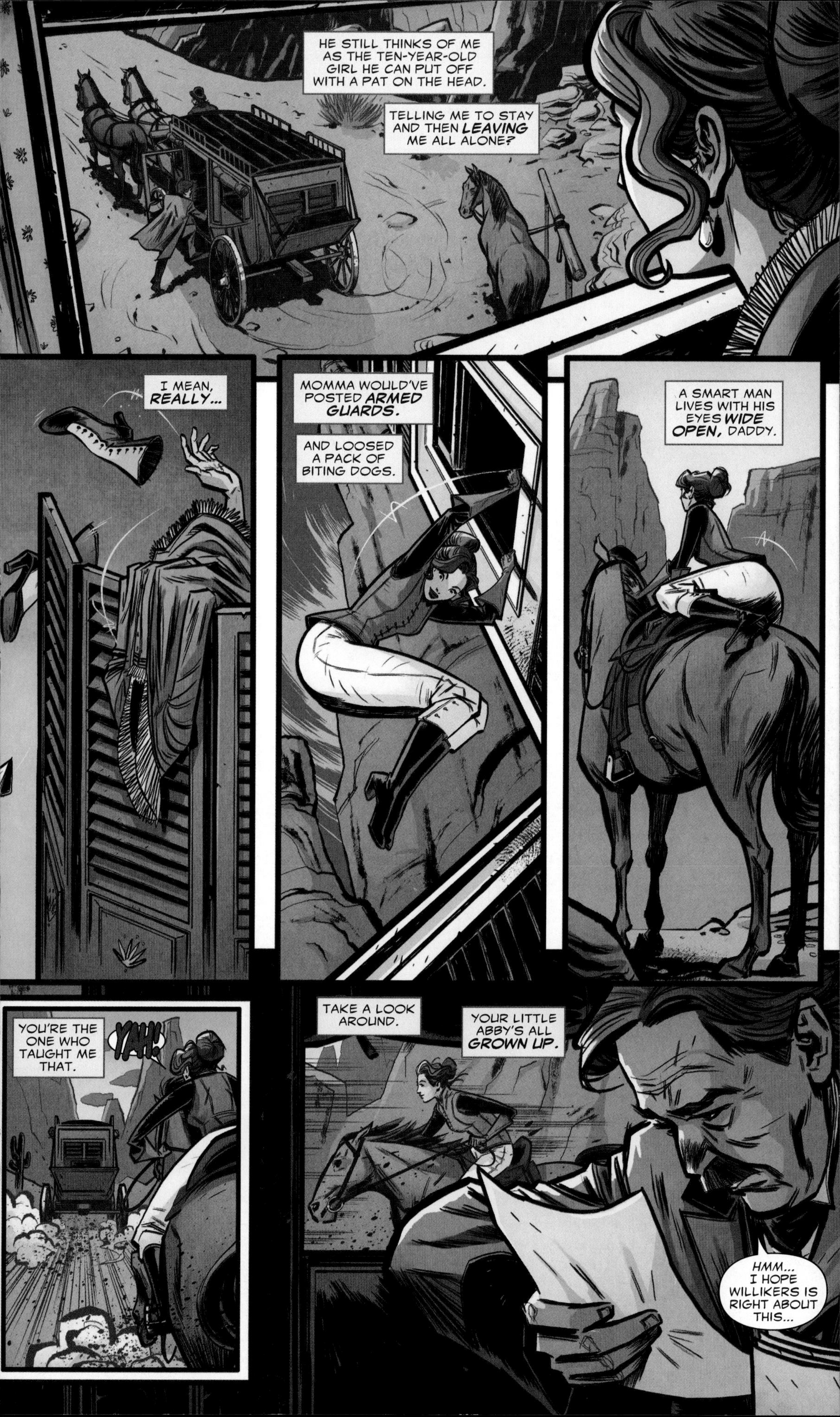
HE STILL THINKS OF ME AS THE TEN-YEAR-OLD GIRL HE CAN PUT OFF WITH A PAT ON THE HEAD.
TELLING ME TO STAY AND THEN LEAVING ME ALL ALONE?
I MEAN, REALLY...
MOMMA WOULD'VE POSTED ARMED GUARDS.
AND LOOSED A PACK OF BITING DOGS.
A SMART MAN LIVES WITH HIS EYES WIDE OPEN, DADDY.
YOU'RE THE ONE WHO TAUGHT ME THAT.
YAH!
TAKE A LOOK AROUND.
YOUR LITTLE ABBY'S ALL GROWN UP.
HMM... I HOPE WILLIKERS IS RIGHT ABOUT THIS...

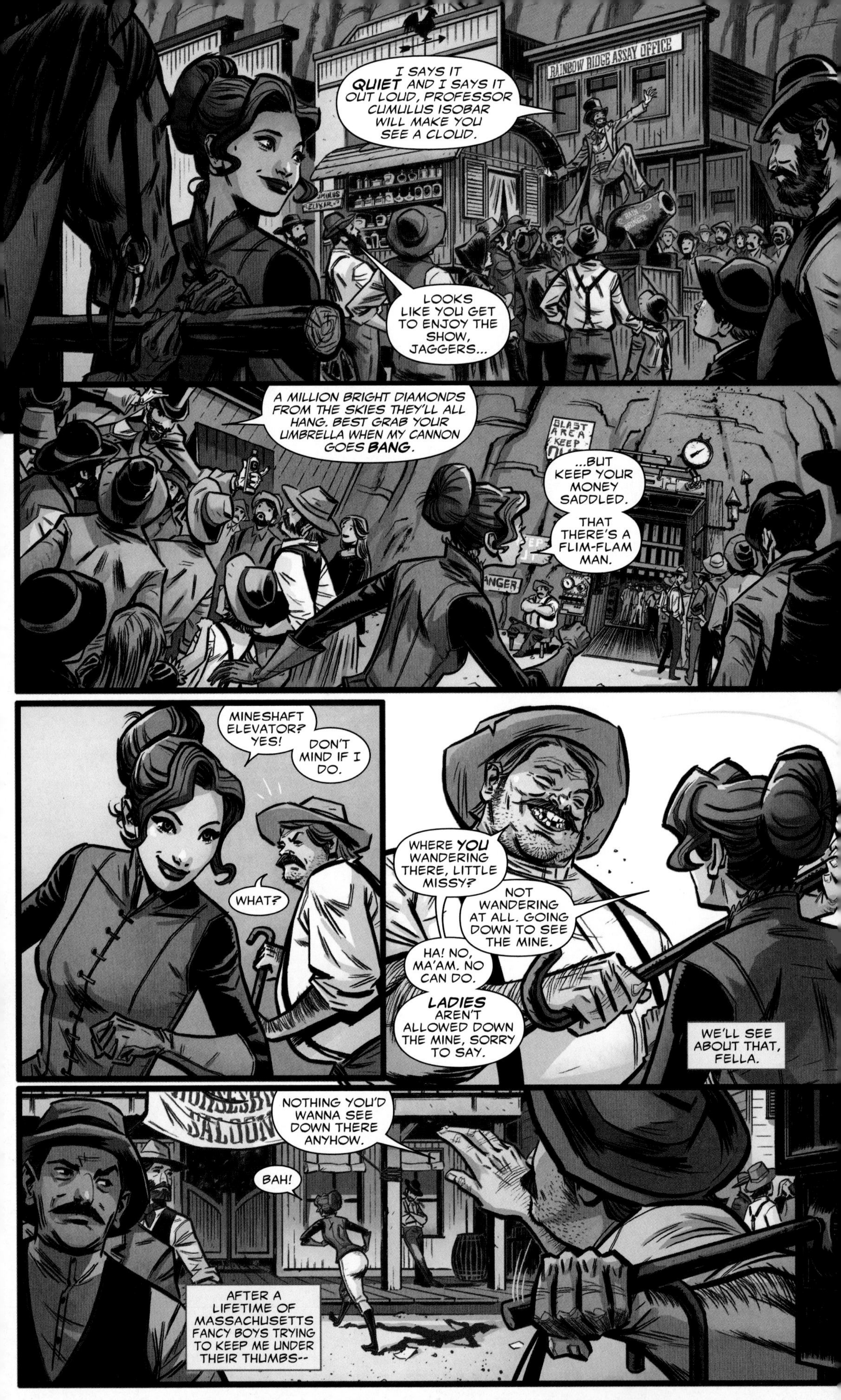

RAINBOW RIDGE ASSAY OFFICE
I SAYS IT QUIET AND I SAYS IT OUT LOUD, PROFESSOR CUMULUS ISOBAR WILL MAKE YOU SEE A CLOUD.
ELIXIR
LOOKS LIKE YOU GET TO ENJOY THE SHOW, JAGGERS...
A MILLION BRIGHT DIAMONDS FROM THE SKIES THEY'LL ALL HANG. BEST GRAB YOUR UMBRELLA WHEN MY CANNON GOES BANG.
...BUT KEEP YOUR MONEY SADDLED.
THAT THERE'S A FLIM-FLAM MAN.
MINESHAFT ELEVATOR? YES!
DON'T MIND IF I DO.
WHAT?
WHERE YOU WANDERING THERE, LITTLE MISSY?
NOT WANDERING AT ALL. GOING DOWN TO SEE THE MINE.
HA! NO, MA'AM. NO CAN DO.
LADIES AREN'T ALLOWED DOWN THE MINE, SORRY TO SAY.
WE'LL SEE ABOUT THAT, FELLA.
SALOON
NOTHING YOU'D WANNA SEE DOWN THERE ANYHOW.
BAH!
AFTER A LIFETIME OF MASSACHUSETTS FANCY BOYS TRYING TO KEEP ME UNDER THEIR THUMBS--

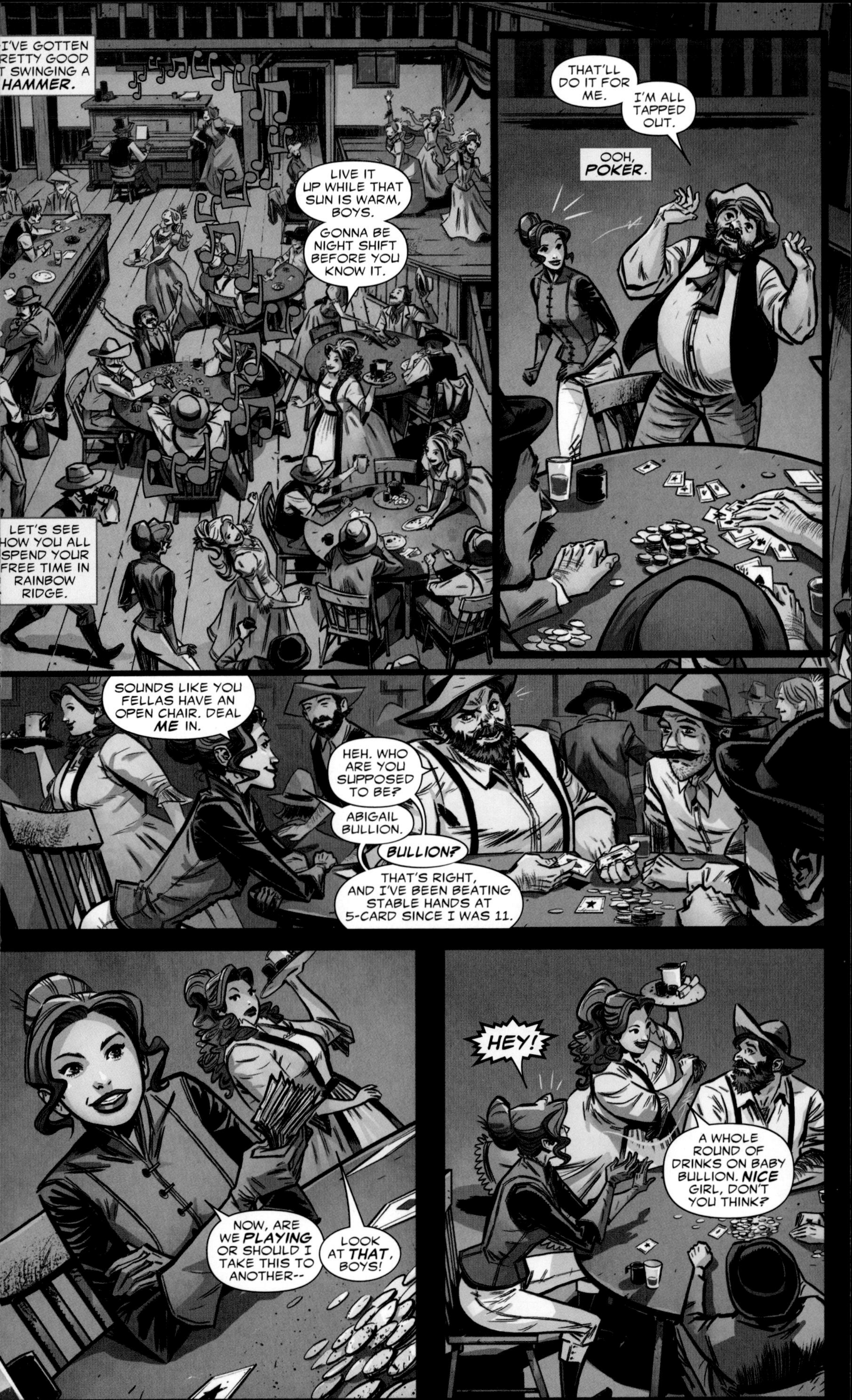

I'VE GOTTEN
RETTY GOOD
T SWINGING A HAMMER.
LIVE IT UP WHILE THAT SUN IS WARM, BOYS.
GONNA BE NIGHT SHIFT BEFORE YOU KNOW IT.
LET'S SEE HOW YOU ALL SPEND YOUR FREE TIME IN RAINBOW RIDGE.
THAT'LL DO IT FOR ME.
I'M ALL TAPPED OUT.
OOH, POKER.
SOUNDS LIKE YOU FELLAS HAVE AN OPEN CHAIR. DEAL ME IN.
HEH. WHO ARE YOU SUPPOSED TO BE?
ABIGAIL BULLION.
BULLION?
THAT'S RIGHT, AND I'VE BEEN BEATING STABLE HANDS AT 5-CARD SINCE I WAS 11.
NOW, ARE WE PLAYING OR SHOULD I TAKE THIS TO ANOTHER--
LOOK AT THAT, BOYS!
HEY!
A WHOLE ROUND OF DRINKS ON BABY BULLION. NICE GIRL, DON'T YOU THINK?

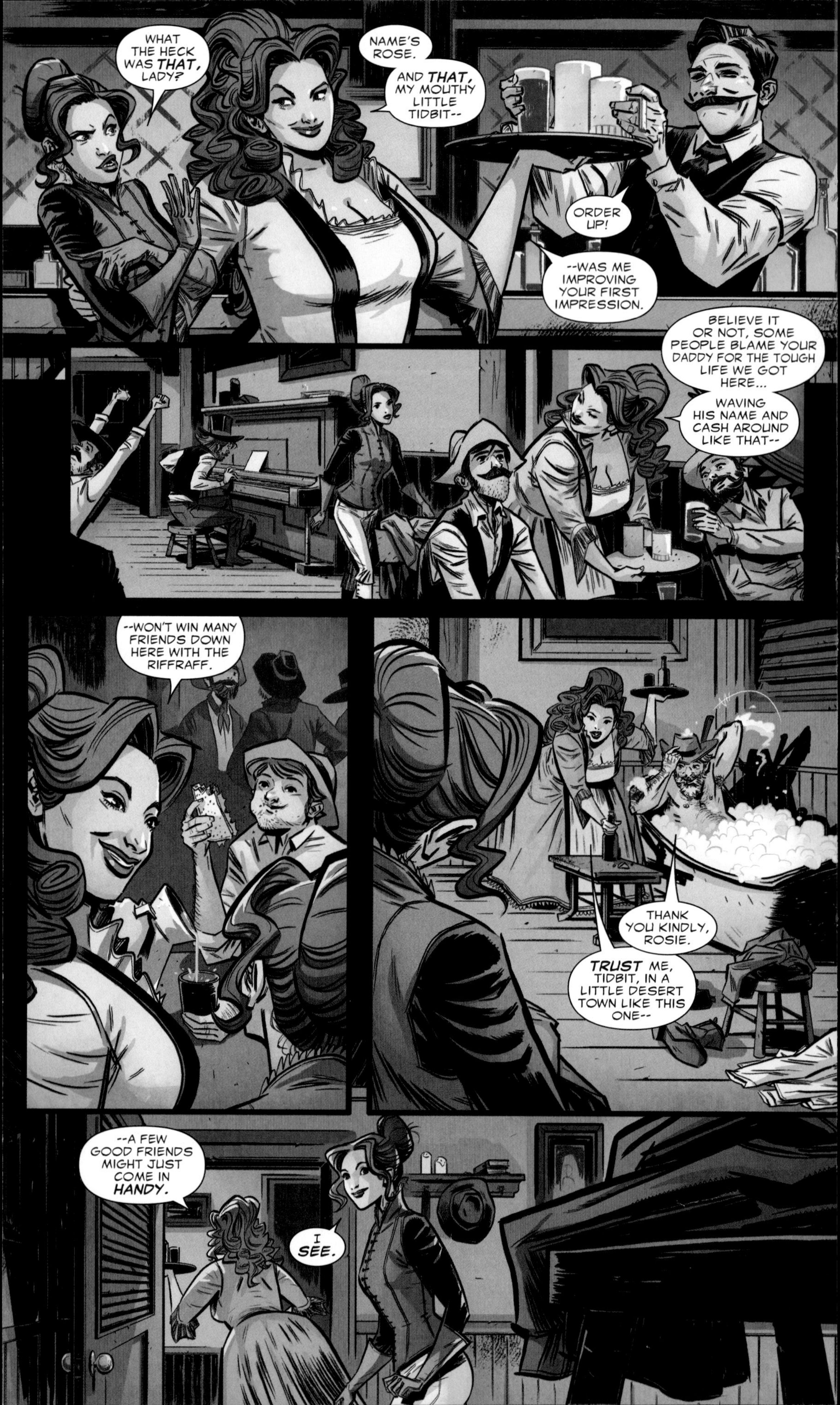
WHAT THE HECK WAS THAT, LADY?
NAME'S ROSE.
AND THAT, MY MOUTHY LITTLE TIDBIT--
ORDER UP!
--WAS ME IMPROVING YOUR FIRST IMPRESSION.
BELIEVE IT OR NOT, SOME PEOPLE BLAME YOUR DADDY FOR THE TOUGH LIFE WE GOT HERE...
WAVING HIS NAME AND CASH AROUND LIKE THAT--
--WON'T WIN MANY FRIENDS DOWN HERE WITH THE RIFFRAFF.
THANK YOU KINDLY, ROSIE.
TRUST ME, TIDBIT, IN A LITTLE DESERT TOWN LIKE THIS ONE--
--A FEW GOOD FRIENDS MIGHT JUST COME IN HANDY.
I SEE.

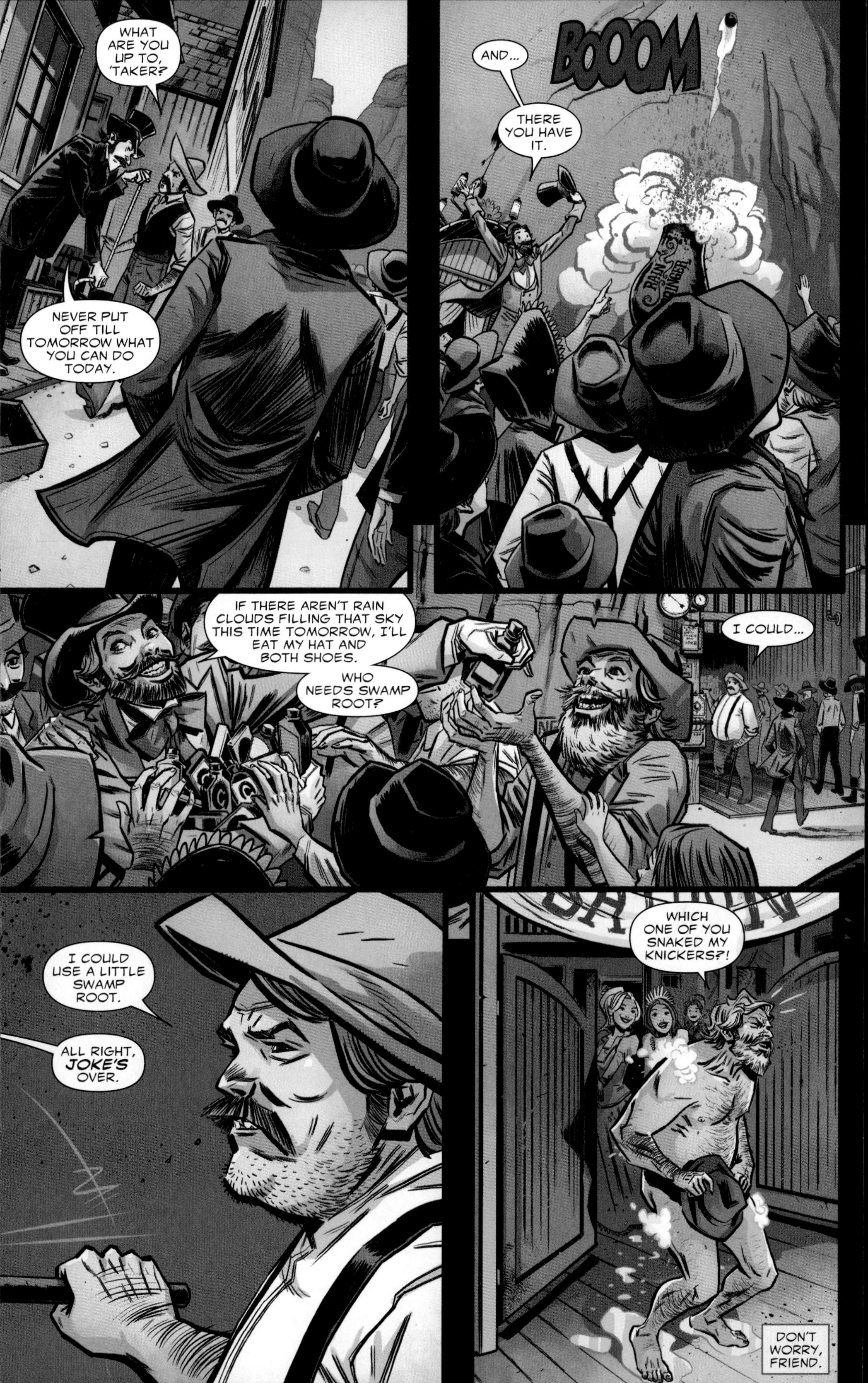
WHAT ARE YOU UP TO, 'TAKER?
NEVER PUT OFF TILL TOMORROW WHAT YOU CAN DO TODAY.
AND...
BOOOM
THERE YOU HAVE IT.
RAIN BRINGER
IF THERE AREN'T RAIN CLOUDS FILLING THAT SKY THIS TIME TOMORROW, I'LL EAT MY HAT AND BOTH SHOES.
WHO NEEDS SWAMP ROOT?
I COULD...
I COULD USE A LITTLE SWAMP ROOT.
ALL RIGHT, **JOKE'S** OVER.
WHICH ONE OF YOU SNAKED MY KNICKERS?!
DON'T WORRY, FRIEND.

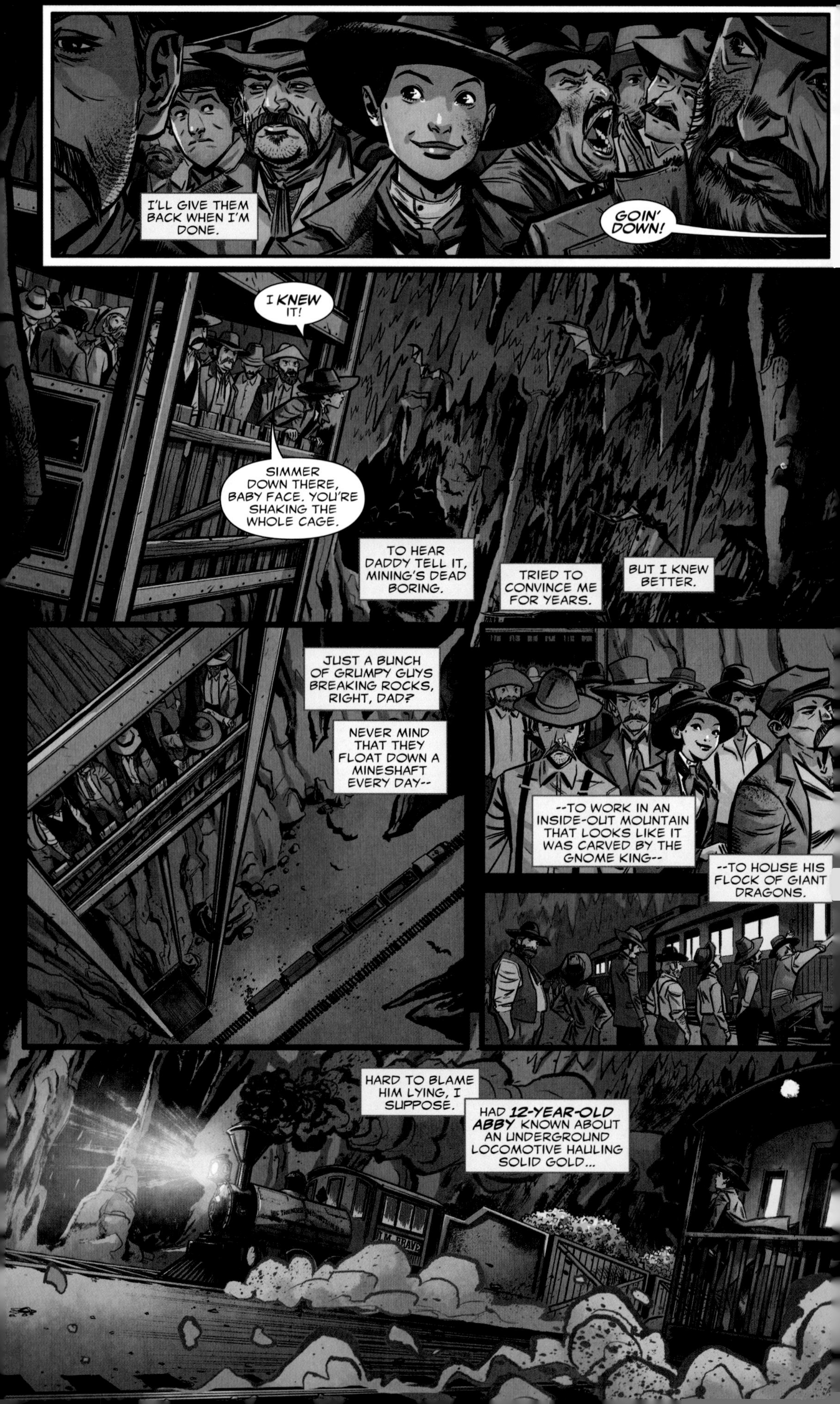
I'LL GIVE THEM BACK WHEN I'M DONE.
GOIN' DOWN!
I KNEW IT!
SIMMER DOWN THERE, BABY FACE. YOU'RE SHAKING THE WHOLE CAGE.
TO HEAR DADDY TELL IT, MINING'S DEAD BORING.
TRIED TO CONVINCE ME FOR YEARS.
BUT I KNEW BETTER.
JUST A BUNCH OF GRUMPY GUYS BREAKING ROCKS, RIGHT, DAD?
NEVER MIND THAT THEY FLOAT DOWN A MINESHAFT EVERY DAY--
--TO WORK IN AN INSIDE-OUT MOUNTAIN THAT LOOKS LIKE IT WAS CARVED BY THE GNOME KING--
--TO HOUSE HIS FLOCK OF GIANT DRAGONS.
HARD TO BLAME HIM LYING, I SUPPOSE.
HAD 12-YEAR-OLD ABBY KNOWN ABOUT AN UNDERGROUND LOCOMOTIVE HAULING SOLID GOLD...

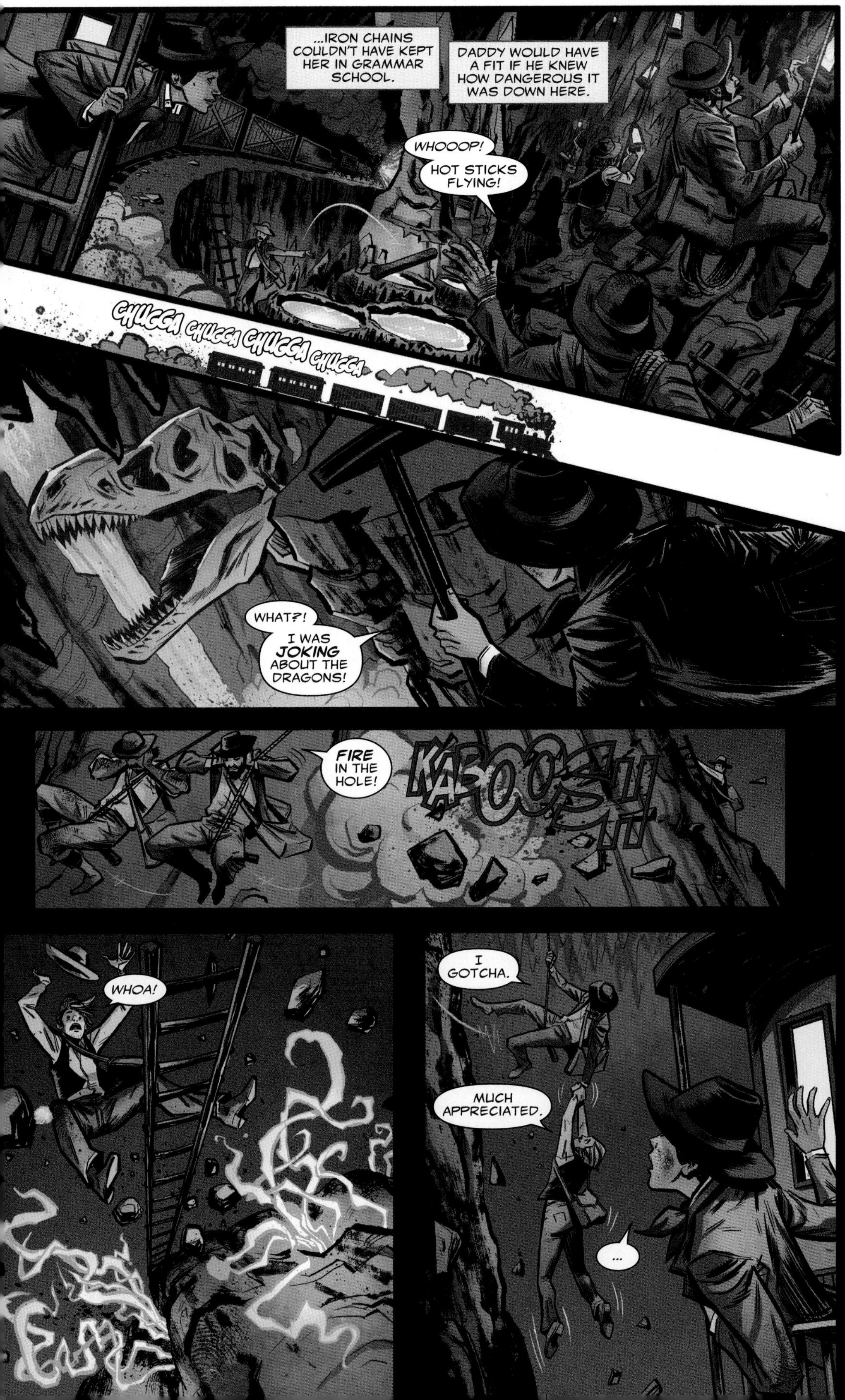
...IRON CHAINS COULDN'T HAVE KEPT HER IN GRAMMAR SCHOOL.
DADDY WOULD HAVE A FIT IF HE KNEW HOW DANGEROUS IT WAS DOWN HERE.
WHOOOP!
HOT STICKS FLYING!
CHUGGA CHUGGA CHUGGA CHUGGA
WHAT?!
I WAS **JOKING** ABOUT THE DRAGONS!
FIRE IN THE HOLE!
KABOOSH!!
WHOA!
I GOTCHA.
MUCH APPRECIATED.
...

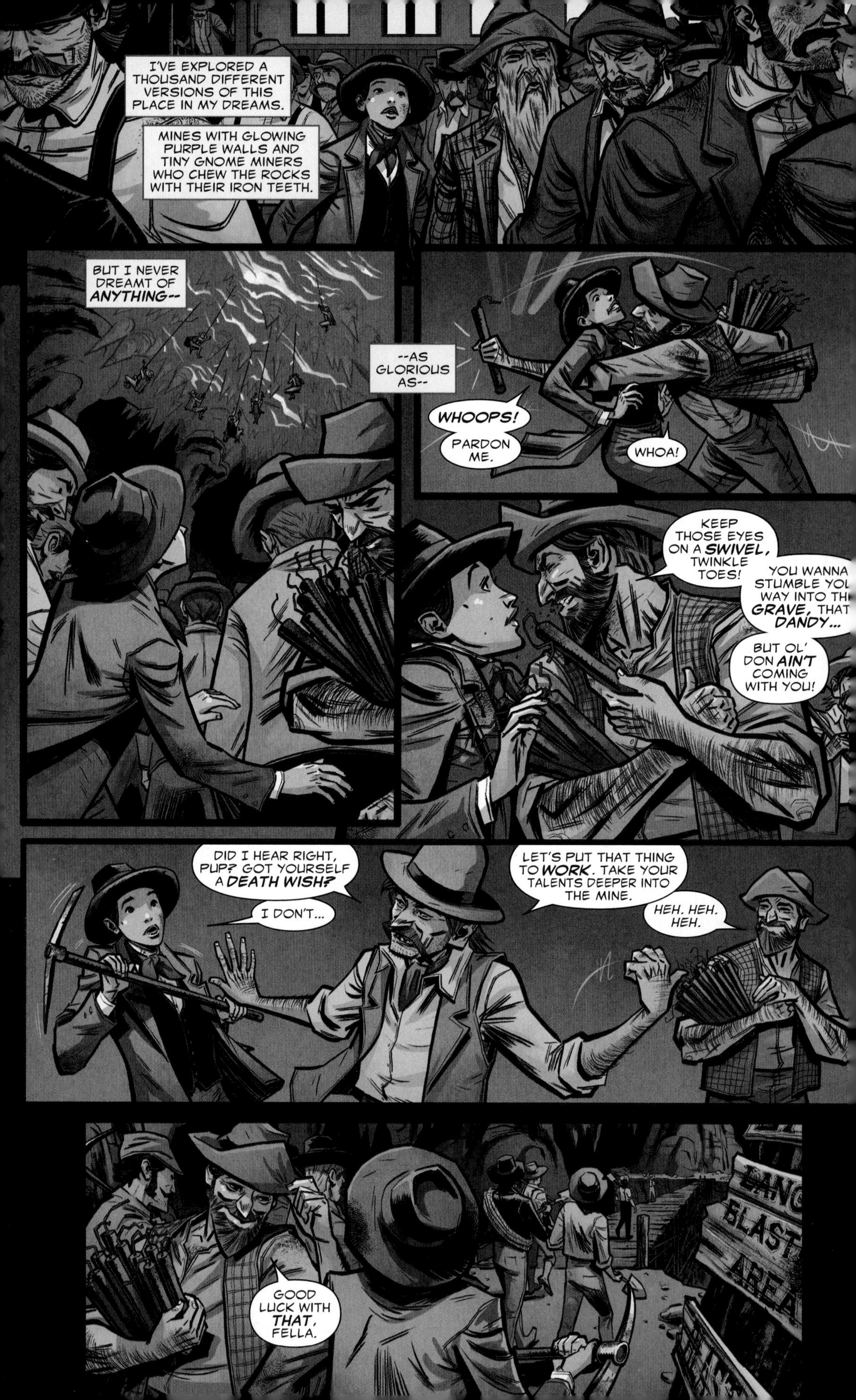

I'VE EXPLORED A THOUSAND DIFFERENT VERSIONS OF THIS PLACE IN MY DREAMS.
MINES WITH GLOWING PURPLE WALLS AND TINY GNOME MINERS WHO CHEW THE ROCKS WITH THEIR IRON TEETH.
BUT I NEVER DREAMT OF ***ANYTHING***--
--AS GLORIOUS AS--
WHOOPS! PARDON ME.
WHOA!
KEEP THOSE EYES ON A ***SWIVEL,*** TWINKLE TOES!
YOU WANNA STUMBLE YOU WAY INTO TH ***GRAVE,*** THAT ***DANDY...***
BUT OL' DON ***AIN'T*** COMING WITH YOU!
DID I HEAR RIGHT, PUP? GOT YOURSELF A ***DEATH WISH?***
I DON'T...
LET'S PUT THAT THING TO ***WORK***. TAKE YOUR TALENTS DEEPER INTO THE MINE.
HEH. HEH. HEH.
BLAST
AREA
GOOD LUCK WITH ***THAT,*** FELLA.

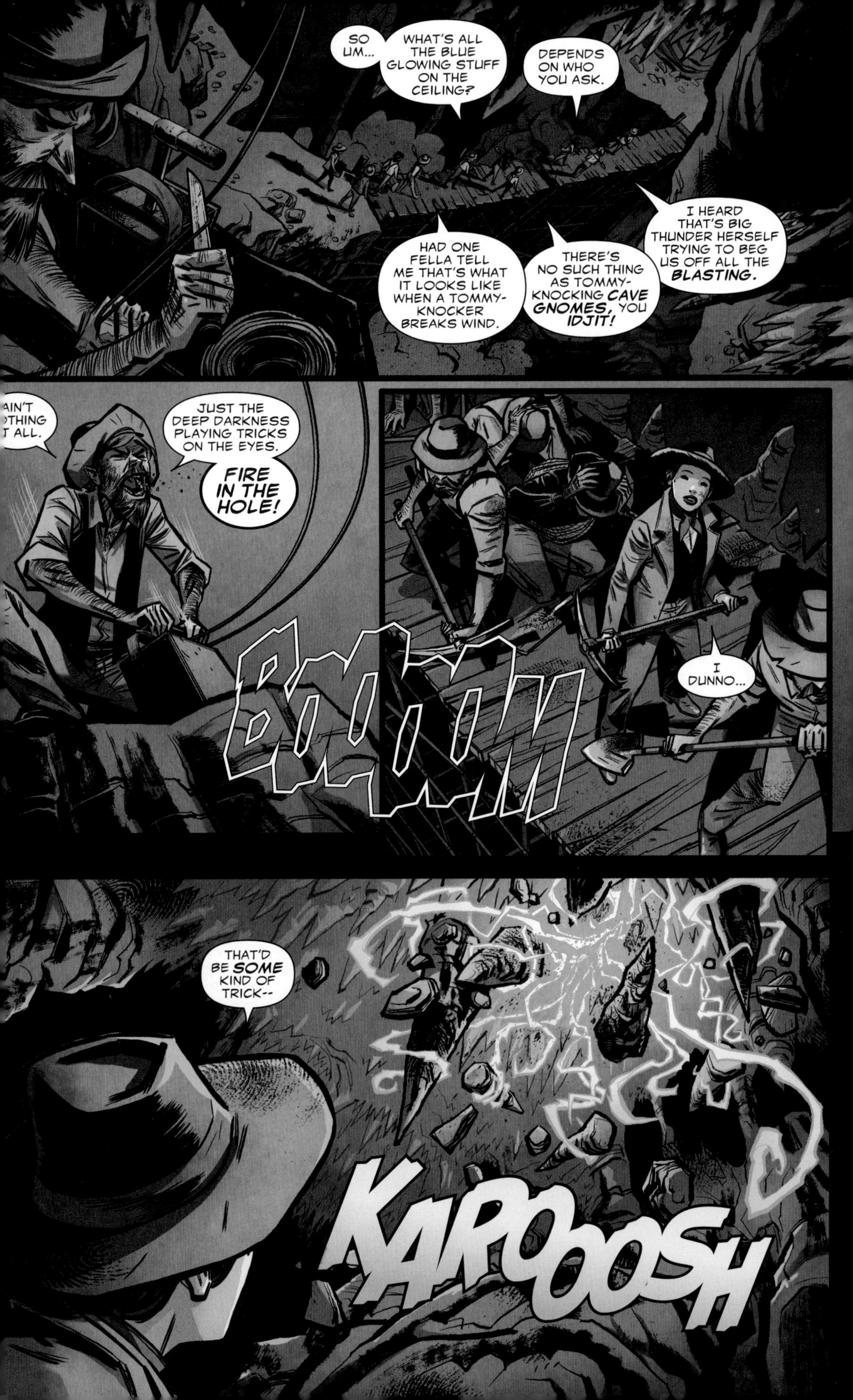
SO UM...
WHAT'S ALL THE BLUE GLOWING STUFF ON THE CEILING?
DEPENDS ON WHO YOU ASK.
HAD ONE FELLA TELL ME THAT'S WHAT IT LOOKS LIKE WHEN A TOMMY-KNOCKER BREAKS WIND.
THERE'S NO SUCH THING AS TOMMY-KNOCKING CAVE GNOMES, YOU IDJIT!
I HEARD THAT'S BIG THUNDER HERSELF TRYING TO BEG US OFF ALL THE BLASTING.
AIN'T OTHING T ALL.
JUST THE DEEP DARKNESS PLAYING TRICKS ON THE EYES.
FIRE IN THE HOLE!
BOOOOM
I DUNNO...
THAT'D BE SOME KIND OF TRICK--
KAPOOOSH

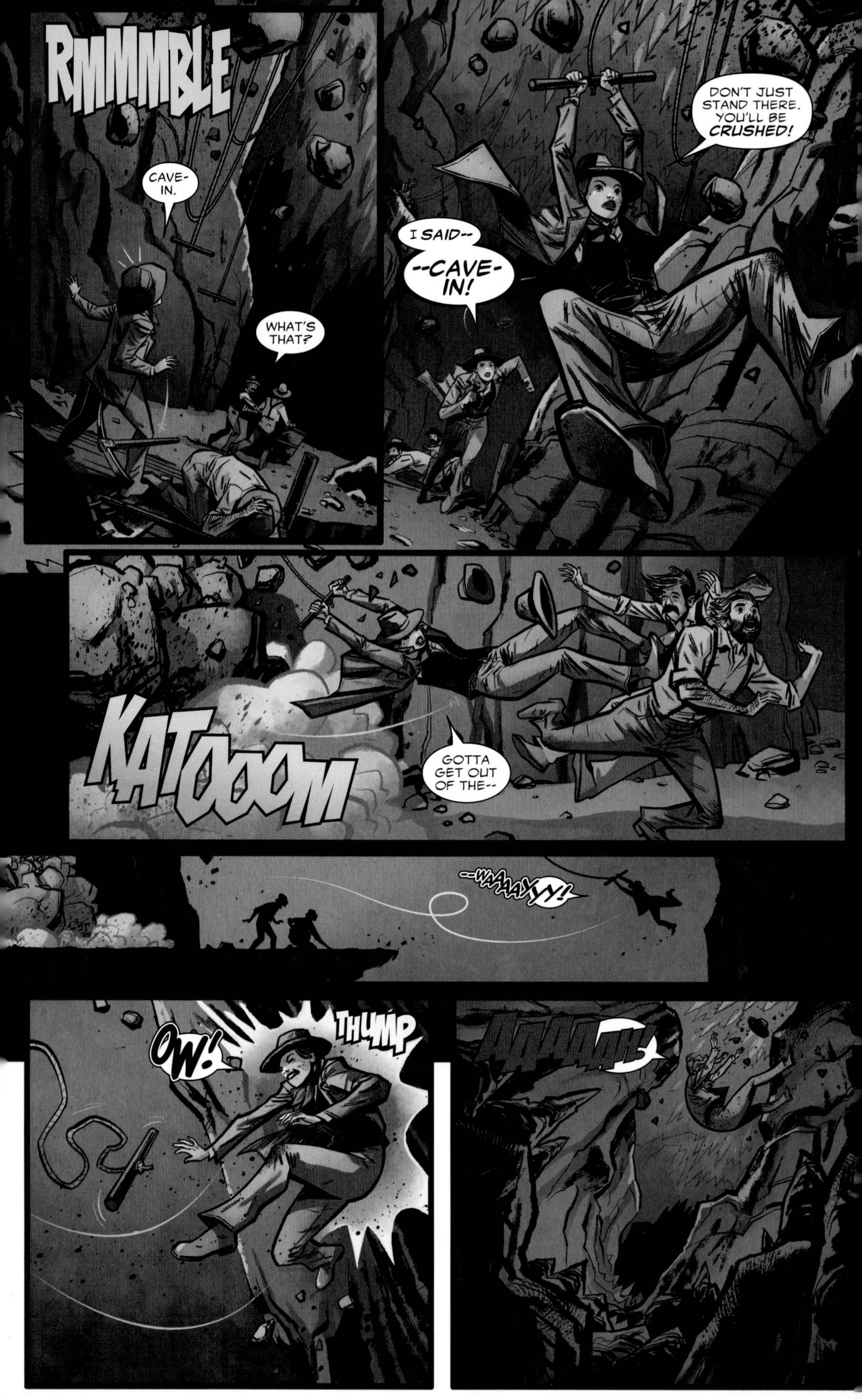
RMMMBLE
CAVE-IN.
WHAT'S THAT?
DON'T JUST STAND THERE. YOU'LL BE CRUSHED!
I SAID--
--CAVE-IN!
KATOOOM
GOTTA GET OUT OF THE--
--WAAAAYYY!
OW!
THUMP

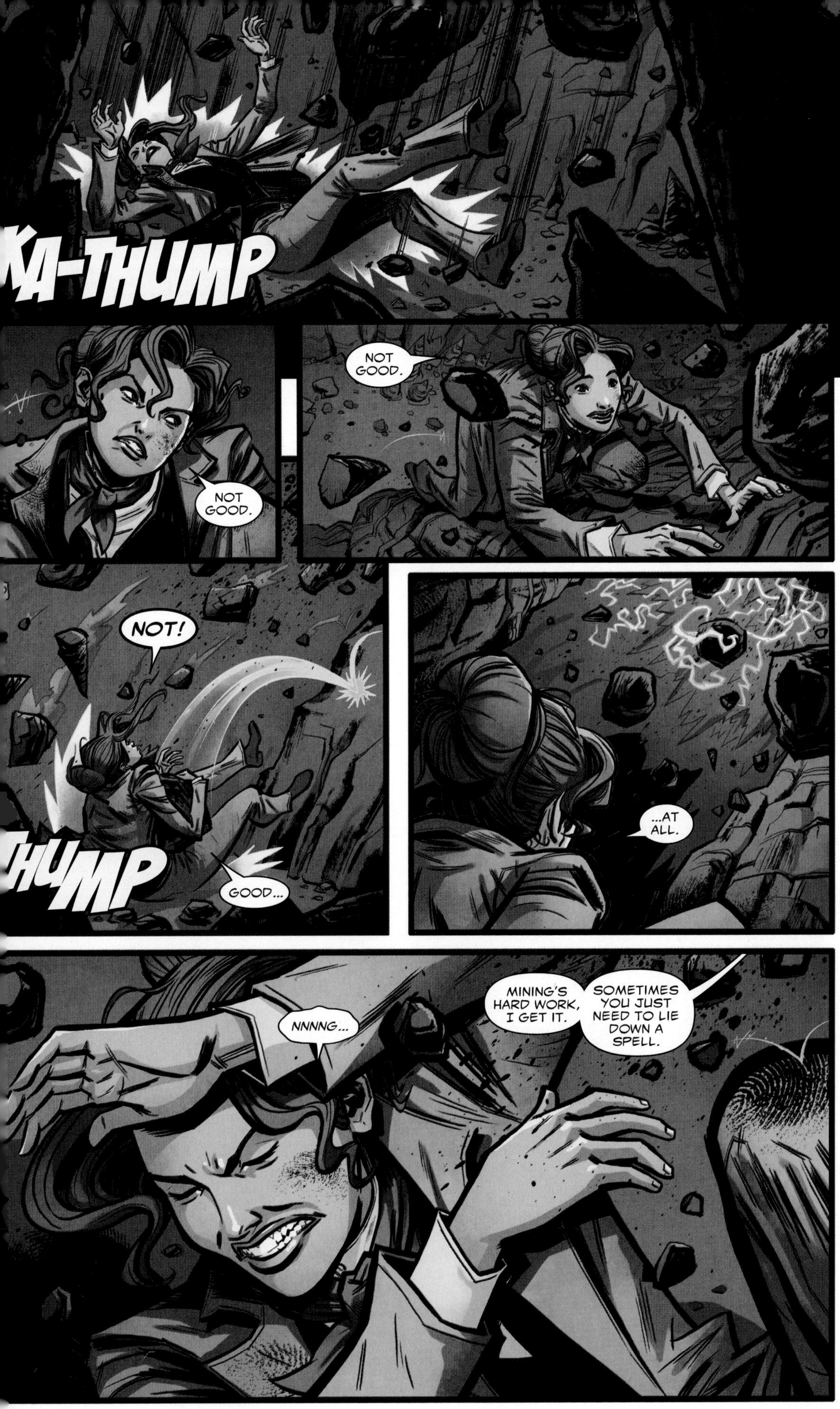
KA-THUMP
NOT GOOD.
NOT GOOD.
NOT!
THUMP
GOOD...
...AT ALL.
NNNNG...
MINING'S HARD WORK, I GET IT.
SOMETIMES YOU JUST NEED TO LIE DOWN A SPELL.

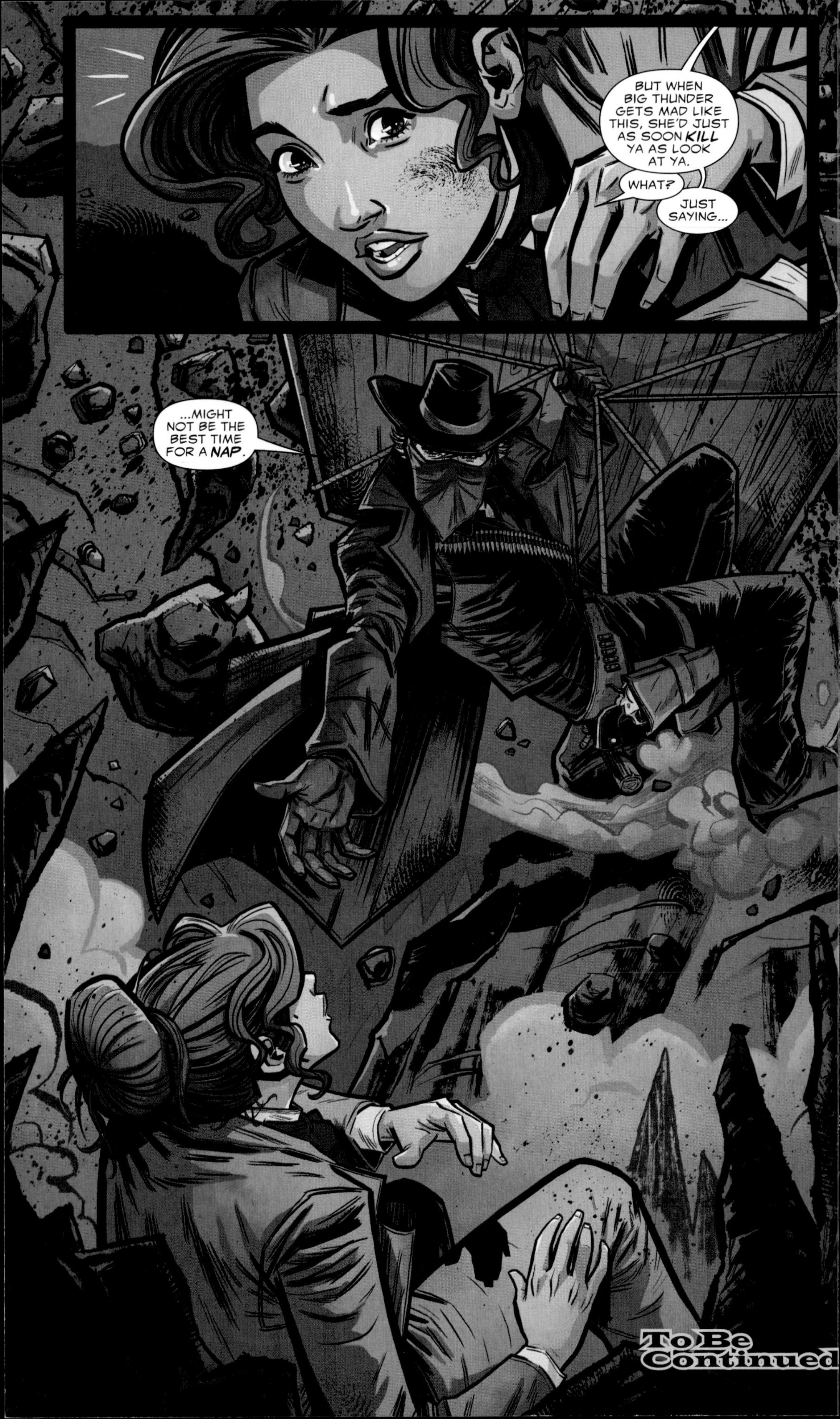
BUT WHEN BIG THUNDER GETS MAD LIKE THIS, SHE'D JUST AS SOON KILL YA AS LOOK AT YA.
WHAT?
JUST SAYING...
...MIGHT NOT BE THE BEST TIME FOR A NAP.
To Be Continued

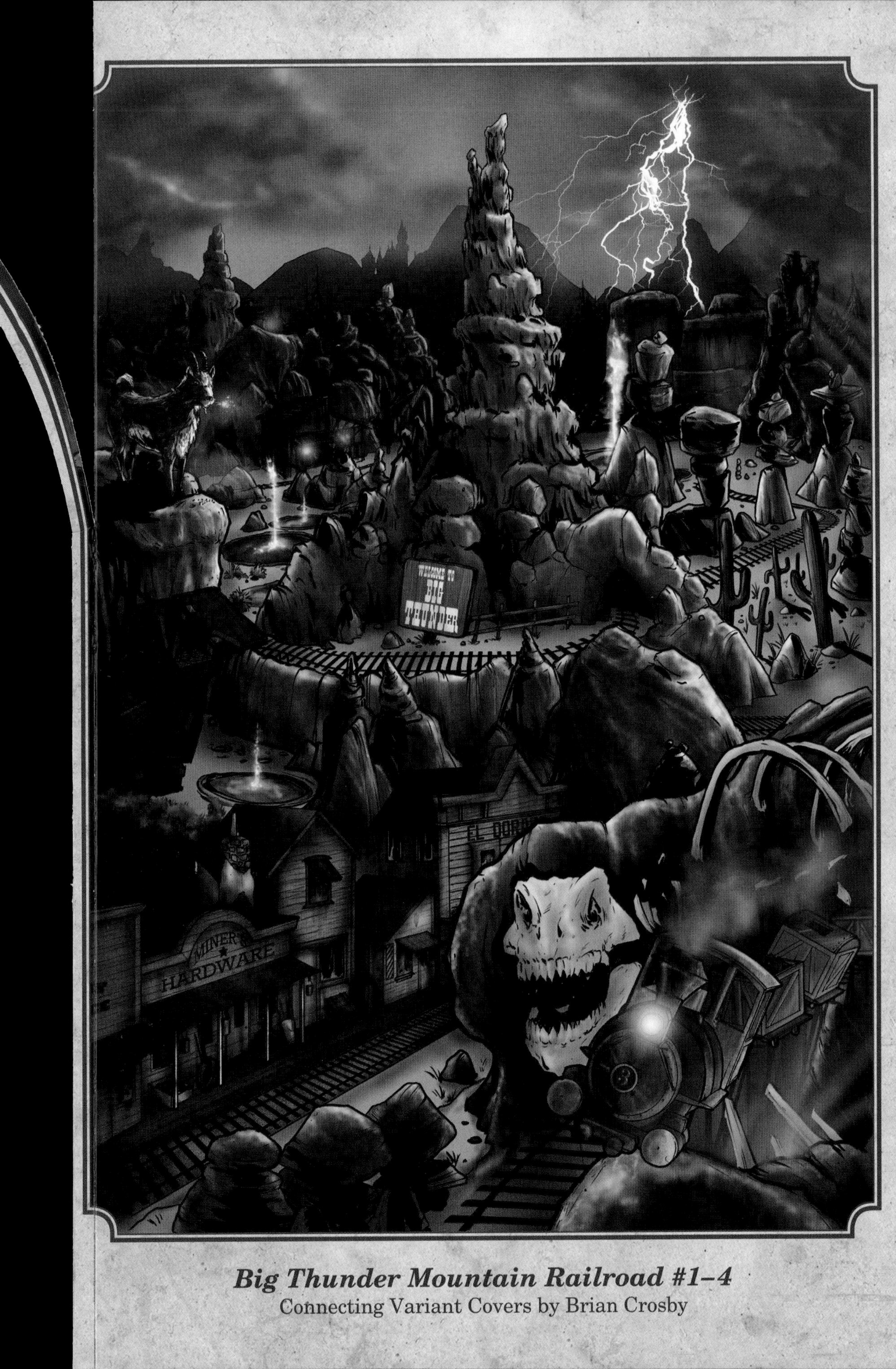
WELCOME TO
BIG
THUNDER
EL DORADO
MINER'S
HARDWARE

Big Thunder Mountain Railroad #1–4
Connecting Variant Covers by Brian Crosby

Disney
KINGDOMS

BIG THUNDER MOUNTAIN RAILROAD

Disney KINGDOMS
BIG THUNDER
MOUNTAIN RAILROAD
MARVEL
HOPELESS
WALKER
BEAULIEU
#1

Hardcover Book ISBN
978-1-61479-575-9

COLLECT THEM ALL!

Set of 5
Hardcover Books ISBN:
978-1-61479-574-2

Disney KINGDOMS
BIG THUNDER
MOUNTAIN RAILROAD
MARVEL
HOPELESS
WALKER
BEAULIEU
#2

Hardcover Book ISBN
978-1-61479-576-6

Disney KINGDOMS
BIG THUNDER
MOUNTAIN RAILROAD
MARVEL
#3

Hardcover Book ISBN
978-1-61479-577-3

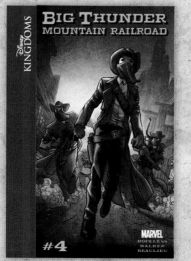

Disney KINGDOMS
BIG THUNDER
MOUNTAIN RAILROAD
MARVEL
HOPELESS
WALKER
BEAULIEU
#4

Hardcover Book ISBN
978-1-61479-578-0

Disney KINGDOMS
BIG THUNDER
MOUNTAIN RAILROAD
MARVEL
HOPELESS
WALKER
MOGORRON
BEAULIEU
#5

Hardcover Book ISBN
978-1-61479-579-7